Audrey is married with four adult children and eight grandchildren. She lives in New Zealand. Being a grandmother has given her a fresh understanding of what is important to children and gave her the impetus for writing Henry Pugh's Wiggly Tooth. Before retiring Audrey worked as a specialist nurse in hospice/palliative care both in New Zealand and in Colorado, USA. She enjoys reading, playing golf, music, movies and travelling with her husband. Most of all she loves spending time with family and friends.

HENRY PUGH'S WIGGLY TOOTH

Audrey Shamy

AUSTIN MACAULEY PUBLISHERS™

LONDON * CAMBRIDGE * NEW YORK * SHARJAH

A CIP catalogue record for this title is available from the British Library.

ISBN 9781528990363 (Paperback)
ISBN 9781528990370 (Hardback)
ISBN 9781528990387 (ePub e-book)

www.austinmacauley.com

First Published (2021)
Austin Macauley Publishers Ltd
25 Canada Square
Canary Wharf
London
E14 5LQ

Dedicated to my grandchildren—William, Jacob, Isaac, Oliver, Evie, Ella, Georgia and James. And to all children everywhere who share the wonder of losing their first teeth.

With love and thanks to my wonderfully supportive husband, Michael, and my children and their partners who read the many revisions of the story with patience and humour! Without their encouragement, the story of Henry Pugh's Wiggly Tooth would never have been written.

One night, in house number six on Bartholomew Street, Henry Pugh sorted his clothes for the morning and got ready for sleep.

He hopped into bed and watched the moon and the stars appear, until his father turned off the light and said, "Sleep time is here."

"Sweet dreams," his father said, leaving the bedroom with Henry tucked up in bed.

But Henry got up, turned on the light and looked in the mirror instead...

He sighed, for despite all his trying, the wiggly tooth was still in his mouth, and he knew the tooth fairy wouldn't leave money, until it was out!

From the kitchen his mother called out in frustration,
"Henry get back into bed right now! NO Negotiation!"
Henry slipped under the covers and gave his tooth one
last tweak. His father called out, "Dream time Henry!"
Soon he was fast asleep.

That night in the silvery moonlight, a tooth fairy eagerly flew to check on the wiggly tooth that belonged to Henry Pugh.

She knew Henry's tooth and had watched it wiggle in class, tonight she was hoping to find his tooth out, waiting in a glass!

Softly calling the tooth's name as she flew to Henry's bed, the tooth was not out as she had hoped_but in his mouth ready for her to inspect!
Although it was quite wobbly, it was still firmly stuck, so the surprised tooth fairy was unhappily...out of luck!

As Henry slept, the tooth fairy appeared in his dream and said encouragingly… "More wriggling, more jiggling and a little more shaking about, is all that's needed now to help that wiggly tooth fall out!"

Next day, Henry told his friends about the tooth fairy dream, "Awesome!" they said, and together they came up with a scheme.

From then on, each day they played with Henry as a team. As he played, Henry worked on loosening his tooth, with the actions suggested by the tooth fairy in his dream. With his friends, Henry played football, did somersaults, handstands and jumped from a tree, while wriggling and jiggling his pesky tooth, as he tried to shake it free.

In the street his friends and family, rode beside Henry on their bikes, cheering and ringing their bells. He rode on his skateboard laughing and twisting his tooth to their yells!

In class, as their teacher read books and sang songs to the beat of a drum, Henry rocked to the rhythm, while moving his tooth round in his gum!

A week had gone by and the tooth fairy wondered, was Henry's tooth still stuck in his mouth?

Or was it waiting in a glass, no longer stuck but out!

She thought about the dream and her suggestions for success.

Yes, she thought, *it was time to fly out and check on its progress!*

Guided by the light of stars, to six Bartholomew Street she flew, thinking about that special tooth that belonged to Henry Pugh.

Peering into Henry's darkened bedroom, her bright eyes saw the glass!

Spinning around and around with glee, she cried out, "At last!"

For there it was, Henry's tooth, all pearly white and shining, the tooth that had wiggled in class, on which she'd been spying!

Collecting the tooth, she danced with fairy delight and was about to fly up out through the roof, and into the night...

But instead she stopped and hovered... "A precious tooth must be paid for," she whispered near Henry's head.

Reaching into her fairy purse she left some money by his bed.

Away she flew into the night leaving something
still to come…
The gift of a permanent tooth, for the gap in
Henry Pugh's gum!

CPSIA information can be obtained
at www.ICGtesting.com
Printed in the USA
BVHW021923210621
610138BV00005B/99

9 781528 990370